The Gaggle Sisters
Sing Again

Written and illustrated by **Chris Jackson**

Lobster Press ™

Jackson, Chris, 1953–
The Gaggle Sisters Sing Again
Text & illustrations © 2003 Chris Jackson

Published by Lobster Press™
1620 Sherbrooke Street West, Suites C & D, Montréal, Québec   H3H 1C9
Tel. (514) 904-1100 • Fax (514) 904-1101 • www.lobsterpress.com

Publisher & Editor: Alison Fripp

Graphic Design & Production: Tammy Desnoyers

"There's a peg on the hat rack of my heart for your sombrero"
Music: Kathryn Briggs 2003 / SOCAN, Lyrics: Chris Jackson

Distributed in the United States by: Distributed in Canada by:
Publishers Group West   Raincoast Books
1700 Fourth Street   9050 Shaughnessey Street
Berkeley, CA 94710   Vancouver, BC V6P 6E5

We acknowledge the financial support of the Government of Canada through the Book Publishing Industry Development Program (BPIDP) for our publishing activities.

The Canada Council | Le Conseil des Arts
for the Arts | du Canada

We acknowledge the support of the Canada Council for the Arts for our publishing program.

National Library of Canada Cataloguing in Publication

Jackson, Chris, 1953-

    The Gaggle sisters sing again / written and illustrated by Chris Jackson.

ISBN 1-894222-56-3

    I. Title.

PS8569.A2525G333 2003   jC813'.54   C2003-902108-4

PZ7

Printed and bound in Korea.

To Len, by the water's edge.

– Chris

Fruit Salad

Last night's concert of the Gaggle Sisters
River Tour had been very successful.
Now, as the sun began to light up the
morning sky, Dorothy could be seen on
the raft, or floating stage as Sadie liked
to call it, shaking a piggy bank.

"Where's the money?" she wondered.
"And where's Sadie?"

Just then Sadie appeared on the bank.

"What do you think? The lady in the shop called it 'Fruit Salad' – isn't it wonderful?" Sadie spun to show off her hat. Around a pale blue brim were:

Apples, Pears, Sugar Plums, Cherries

Passion Fruit, Grapefruit, Assorted Berries

Clementines, Apricots, Granny Smith's. Kumquats

Tangerines, Nectarines and two Banana What-nots

Dorothy realized where all the money had gone.

"Sadie!" said Dorothy.
"We can't afford new hats. We need to eat."

"Oh Dorothy – you are such a
grouch," said Sadie admiring herself
in a mirror. "You know I can't resist a beautiful
hat. And anyway, we'll make money at
the next show – people will come just
to see me in this hat – now don't
you worry."

"But what will we eat in the meantime?"
Dorothy's frown turned
into slow smile. "I know,
we can eat your hat."

"Now, now, Dorothy don't be – "
Sadie was suddenly interrupted
by a loud *BOOM* overhead.
A crack of thunder split the sky
and it began to rain.
Sadie, screaming about her
hat, ran this way and that
way in panic. Finally she
ducked into the tent.

The Bridge

The rain quickly turned to a downpour.
Dorothy realized she would have to find
shelter quickly. She looked around frantically.
That was when she saw the bridge.
"Perfect!" she said, and began
poling as hard as she could. The
bridge was some distance down river,
and by the time the raft slipped
beneath it, Dorothy was
soaked to the skin. The
gloom underneath the
bridge matched her
mood.

"C'mon Dorothy – you know how I hate it when you're angry with me," said Sadie. "Let me sing you something."

"How about *'the soaking wet accordion player'* ?" suggested Dorothy grimly.

"I don't think I know that one," frowned Sadie. "No, I was thinking more about a little hat medley."

Sadie sang half a dozen 'hat' songs, finishing with *"There's a peg on the hat rack of my heart for your sombrero"* – a fast Mexican number and one of Dorothy's favorites.

The echoes under the bridge added sweetness to Sadie's voice.

Dorothy was beginning to feel better. She got out her accordion and accompanied Sadie.

Suddenly Sadie stopped singing. "Hey! It's stopped raining," she announced, and then added, "what's that crowd doing in the water?"

Dorothy looked to where she was pointing.

"Those are reflections," she laughed and poled the raft out from under the bridge.

The two performers were met with applause. Sadie and Dorothy bowed as money rained down onto the raft. Sadie held out her hat which soon became full.

"You see, I told you not to worry," said Sadie. "You know, there's enough money here to buy a new hat."

Dorothy scowled at her.

" . . . for you," Sadie added quickly.

The Frog

The following morning Sadie shook Dorothy awake. Eyes wide with fear, she pointed to a large shadow on the side of the tent.

"Wha-wha-what's that?"

"It looks like a thingama-bob but rounder," said Dorothy. "It's too small for a whatchama-call-it, too big for a something-or-other."

"I don't care what it is," hissed Sadie. "Go and see what it wants!"

The sun was very bright and Dorothy had trouble seeing anything at first.

"Er . . . Hello?" she said.

She looked around but there was no thingama-bob. No whatchama-call-it. No something-or-other. But there was a frog.

"It's a frog," said Dorothy

"I can see that," said Sadie grumpily. "Ask him what he thinks he's doing – disturbing decent folk at this hour of the day."

"What can we do for you?" asked Dorothy. The frog said nothing but held out a clam.

"Is there something inside?" she asked. The frog opened the clam. Suddenly the air was filled with a simple, haunting piece of music. The tune wafted in the air long enough for Dorothy to catch its drift. She hummed it to herself as she took up her accordion. Quickly she found the tune among the keys.

As Dorothy played, the frog began to dance.

"He dances like a thingama-bob but better.
Like a whatchama-call-it but with more grace.
Like a something-or-other but with style,"
said Dorothy.

"He's all right," said Sadie reluctantly,
and then added, "for a frog."
  "I know!" announced Dorothy.
"He could be in the show – and
with this music – it'll be great!"

Shadows

"Just a moment!" said Sadie, puffing out her chest. "*Artistes* like myself do not appear with mere frogs."

"But Sadie," pleaded Dorothy, "the little fellow is so talented."

"It wouldn't matter if he had all the talent in the world," argued Sadie. "Apart from anything else – he's simply too small."

Dorothy had to admit the frog *was* small. "He looked so big when he was a shadow on the tent this morning," thought Dorothy.

Then suddenly an idea came to her, bright and shiny. "I know."

"I'm warning you, Dorothy, I am not sharing the stage with a frog," stated Sadie. "Do I make myself clear?"

"Crystal clear."

At the concert that night, Sadie sang, Dorothy played the accordion – and the little frog danced. Being careful not to dance too near the flame, the little frog gave a great performance. Sadie, unaware of the shadow dancing on the backdrop behind her, sang all the better for the cheers from the audience.

After the show Dorothy found the little frog about to jump from the end of the raft. "Can't you stay?" she asked.
The frog shook his head.
"Then take this with you," said Dorothy. She whispered, "You are a great dancer" into the clam, before closing it tight. Then plop, the frog disappeared beneath the dark waters of the river.

Just then Sadie appeared.
"Did you hear them tonight, Dorothy?
They loved me."